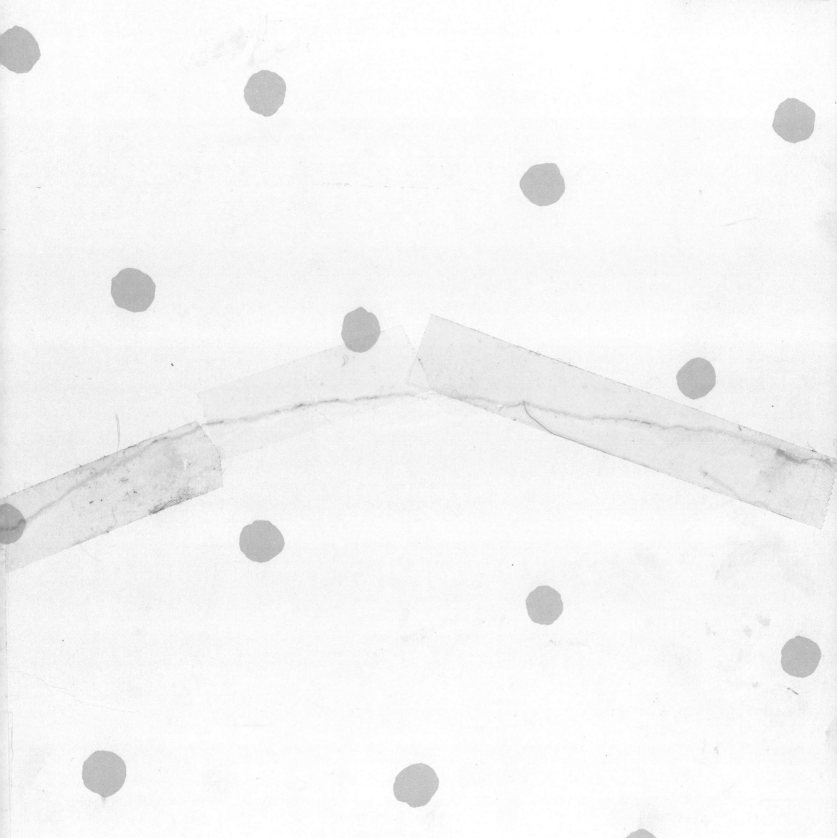

RUBY'S POTTY

by Paul & Emma Rogers
Dutton Children's Books • New York

For Ruby — who else!

Text copyright © 2001 by Paul Rogers
Illustrations copyright © 2001 by Emma Rogers
All rights reserved.

CIP Data is available.

Published in the United States 2001 by Dutton Children's Books,
a division of Penguin Putnam Books for Young Readers
345 Hudson Street, New York, New York 10014
www.penguinputnam.com

Originally published in Great Britain 2001 by Orchard Books, London
Typography by Jason Henry
Printed in Singapore

First American Edition
1 3 5 7 9 10 8 6 4 2
ISBN 0-525-46816-1

Ruby's got a potty.

She rides it round the floor.

The trouble is, she doesn't know
just what a potty's for.

She hides it . . .

She slides it . . .

She puts it
on her head.

And when it's nearly nighttime,

she makes it Rabbit's bed.

She takes it to
the playground.

She takes it to the park.

It's handy in
the sandbox.

For carrying
things, it's great.

But when it's really needed —

Where is it?

Oops!

Too late.

"No diaper on," says Ruby.
"No diaper anymore."

(But still she doesn't really know just what a potty's for.)

She stays on it for ages.

Then "Look!" calls Ruby. "Look!"

But all she's showing Daddy
is something in her book.

She sits her teddies, one by one,

around it in a ring.

When Mommy sits *her* on it, though,

she never
does a thing.

She puts it in her wagon

and pushes
it around.

But when it's time for dinner,

she's nowhere to be found.

She isn't in the playhouse

or underneath the tree.

Then "Come and look!" calls Ruby,

with potty at the door.

Hooray!

Now Ruby really knows
just what a potty's for!